Pack it

Written by Fiona Tomlinson
Photographed by Will Amlot

Collins

Kim picks the dogs.

Dad packs the tops.

Kim picks a cot.

Dad packs the socks.

Kim picks a man.

Dad packs the pot.

Kim picks a pan.

Dad packs the map.

Kim picks the cats.

Dad packs the kit.

Kim picks a dog.

Dog

Dad packs in the dog.

/c/

❧ After reading ❧

Letters and Sounds: Phase 2

Word count: 50

Focus phonemes: /g/ /o/ /c/ /k/ ck

Common exception words: the, and

Curriculum links: Understanding the World; Personal, Social and Emotional development

Early learning goals: Reading: read and understand simple sentences; use phonic knowledge to decode regular words and read them aloud accurately; demonstrate understanding when talking with others about what they have read

Developing fluency

- Your child may enjoy hearing your read the story to model fluency and rhythm in the book.

Phonic practice

- Ask your child to sound talk and blend each of the following words: c/o/t, p/o/t, d/u/ck, d/o/g, p/i/ck/s
- Look at the repeated words **picks** and **packs** and discuss the phoneme that is different in the two words (/i/ and /a/). Practise sounding out and blending both words and listening to the difference.
- Look at the "I spy sounds" pages (14–15). Discuss the picture with your child. Can they find items/ examples of words that contain the /c/ and /k/ sounds? (e.g. *camera, camping, cake, car, cup, cool box, kettle, kid, ketchup, kit, Kim*)

Extending vocabulary

- Kim **picks** toys to take camping. What words could you use instead of **picks**? (e.g. *chooses, selects, wants, prefers, requests*)
- Dad and Kim are going on a camping **holiday**. What words could you use instead of **holiday**? (e.g. *vacation, break, trip, journey, weekend away, outing, tour, getaway, excursion, adventure, sleepover*)
- Dad and Kim pack their things into a **rucksack**. What else could you pack your things into? (e.g. a *suitcase, luggage, shopping bag, kitbag, briefcase, backpack, schoolbag*)